D0192090

THIS BOOK BELONGS TO

....

Old Father Christmas

First published in Great Britain
by HarperCollins Publishers Ltd in 1993
10 9 8 7 6 5 4 3 2 1
First published in Picture Lions in 1994
10 9 8 7 6 5 4 3 2 1
Picture Lions is an imprint of the Children's Division,
part of HarperCollins Publishers Limited,
77-85 Fulham Palace Road, Hammersmith,
London W6 8JB

ISBN 0 00 185424 0 (Hardback)
ISBN 0 00 674158 4 (Picture Lions)
Text copyright © Berlie Doherty 1993
Illustrations copyright © Maria Teresa Meloni 1993

Produced by HarperCollins Hong Kong
This book is set in 16/24 Galliard

Old Father Christmas

Based on a story by Juliana Horatia Ewing
and retold by Berlie Doherty

Illustrated by Maria Teresa Meloni

PictureLions
An Imprint of HarperCollins*Publishers*

OLD FATHER CHRISTMAS

If you know a very old lady who likes to tell you stories, then she might have told you about a very old man who used to tell her stories when she was a little girl. His name might be Godfather Garbel. The story she loved to hear most was the one about Old Father Christmas.

Listen, and you might just be able to hear Godfather Garbel telling her the story. Can you see him winking in the firelight? Can you see him shuffling his feet backwards and forwards in his square shoes as he's talking? You can hear the leather squeaking half a room away.

He's telling her about when he was a little boy, years and years before you were born, years and years before the old lady was born. He's telling her about the best Christmas he ever had.

• CHAPTER ONE •

WHEN GODFATHER GARBEL WAS A LITTLE BOY

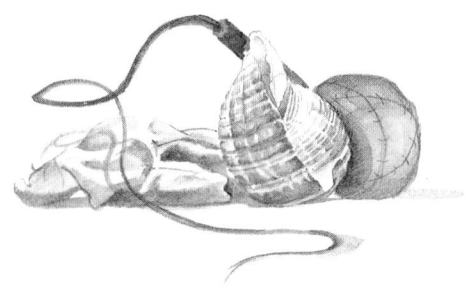

Can you imagine, he says, that once upon a time I was a little boy? I used to have a Godmother too, and she used to give me presents. I'm going to tell you about the present she gave me for my eighth birthday.

Children didn't get the sort of presents then that they get now.

Grrmph! They did not!

We didn't get half the presents you get, but we kept them twice as long. And I think we loved them more than you love your presents.

Grrmph! I think we did!

I'll tell you what I got on my eighth birthday.

My mother knitted me a blue scarf.

My little sister Patty gave me a ball that she'd made out of rags and stuffed with bran and bits of cork.

My father gave me a broken whip and a pair of old gloves, so I could pretend to be the driver of a coach

and horses! How I loved them! How I rode round and round the yard, cracking my whip and stretching out my fingers in those cracked old gloves!

And Kitty gave me a shell that had the voice of the sea inside it. I could hold it up to my ear and listen to the sea roaring. I'd never seen the sea.

"Does it really sound like this?" I asked Kitty, pressing the shell to my ear.

"Yes, it does," she promised me. "It roars and whispers, just like that."

I made everyone in the house listen to it, even Puss, the stripy old cat. I saw Dick from the village go past the window with a pile of straw for stuffing Guy Fawkes with and I raced out with the shell in my hand so he would hear the sea too. I gave him such a fright when I pushed it against his ear that he turned round and knocked me over with his pile of straw.

"Now what did you go and do that for?" he asked me. He was a bit upset because I'd made him jump.

"I wanted you to hear the sea in my shell," I told him. I was a bit upset, too, because he'd pushed me into a puddle.

So Dick picked me up and rubbed me down and gave me two and a half sticks of treacle straight out of his pocket, and I let him listen to the shell, and told him he could listen to the sea roaring in it every Saturday afternoon from now on.

Now weren't they wonderful presents? And still I

hadn't had a present from my godmother. At last it came, on the evening coach, a parcel for me from my godmother.

It was a picture book. She'd drawn all the pictures herself, and coloured them in, and she'd written little rhyming stories about the characters. They were all about people like Guy Fawkes. And the Man in the Moon. And Punch. And there was one about Old Father Christmas. And that's where my story begins.

· CHAPTER TWO ·

THE PICTURE BOOK

My sister Patty was six years old. We loved each other very much. The picture book was almost as much hers as mine. We used to sit on a big stool by the fire with our arms round each other and the book resting on our knees.

"My word," said Kitty. "If books were always as good as that, I wouldn't mind having one myself!"

Patty and I loved all the pictures, but the one of Old Father Christmas took our hearts by storm. We'd never seen anything like him, you see. These days you can buy plaster models of him from any toy-shop at Christmastime, but we'd never seen him before, and there he was, with his long white hair and his beard like cotton wool. And he was carrying a Christmas tree.

Well, let me tell you, I'd never seen a Christmas tree in my life before! The first picture I ever saw of one was when I was eight years old, and it was carried by Old

Father Christmas in my godmother's picture book. I couldn't stop looking at it.

"What are those things on the tree?" I asked my father.

"Candles," he said.

But there were other things that were even more exciting than candles.

"What are those coloured things?" I asked him.

"Toys," he said.

I looked at Patty.

"Are they ever taken off?" I hardly dared to ask him that.

"Yes! They're taken off and given to the children who stand round the tree."

Patty and I held each other's hands tightly. "Isn't Father Christmas kind!" we both said.

We gazed at the picture again.

"How old is Old Father Christmas?" I asked.

My father laughed. "He's one thousand eight hundred and thirty years old," he told us. "Because that's how long it is since the very first Christmas day."

And that was the very year we were in, when I was only eight years old.

"He looks very old," whispered Patty. "Very, very old."

Well, November went by, and December went by, and still we loved to look at the picture book. We looked at the picture of Old Father Christmas so often that he was like a friend. We felt as if we really knew him, and that if we ever saw him we would recognise him straight away. But has anybody ever really seen Old Father Christmas?

Christmas week came, and Christmas Eve came. My mother and father were mysteriously busy in the front room, and Patty and I weren't allowed to go in. We went into the kitchen, but there was no place of rest for us even there.

"Go away," Kitty told us. "I'm all over the place, can't you see?"

It looked as if the cakes, mince pies and Christmas puddings were all over the place with her, too.

"There's no room here for children sitting with their toes in the fire reading books!" she told us. "The cat's quite enough, thank you!"

With that she gave Puss a little kick with her slipper that was meant to send her flying like a football away from the fireplace. It was a hint to her to get out of the way into the Christmas frost, but Puss didn't take the hint at all. Every time it happened she would always creep softly back to her warm place on the hearth.

But we weren't as brave as Puss. We put Kitty's shawl over our heads and went outside.

"Perhaps we'll see Dick," I said.

But Dick was busy helping his father to decorate the church. In those days they used to make little holes at both ends of all the church benches and stick sprigs of holly in them. You had to be very careful not to scratch your nose on them when you sat down.

We ran across the yard and looked over the wall to see if there was anything interesting there. Behind the wall was a long field where flowers grew in summer, and it sloped up to a hill that was so windy that people used to go there to cure their whooping-cough.

It was nearly as good as going to the seaside. And today it looked strange, all covered with snow and standing off against the grey sky. The white fields looked vast and dreary in the dusk, but there was a holly hedge, bright with berries, and a fat robin redbreast staring at me. I stared back at the robin. Patty was peeping out of the other end of Kitty's shawl, and she suddenly gave a great jump that dragged it from our heads and cried,

"Look!"

• CHAPTER THREE •

OLD FATHER CHRISTMAS

I looked. An old man was coming along the lane. His hair and beard were as white as cotton wool. He had a face like the sort of apple that keeps well in winter; his coat was old and brown. There were patches of snow on him, and he was carrying a little fir tree.

Patty and I both had the same thought.

"It's Old Father Christmas!" we breathed.

What we didn't know then was that he was an old man from the village who was taking the fir tree up to the Hall, to be made into a Christmas tree. He was a cheerful old fellow, and rather deaf. He made up for this by nodding his head all the time and smiling and saying, "Aye, aye, to be sure!" every now and again.

As he passed us he saw us looking at him and smiled up in such a friendly way that I was brave enough to say, "Hello, Father Christmas!" to him.

"Same to you!" he said, in a high-pitched voice.

"So you ARE Father Christmas!" said Patty.

"And a Happy New Year!" was his reply, which puzzled me a bit, I must say. But he smiled so cheerfully that Patty went on, "You're very old, aren't you?"

"So I be, Miss, so I be," nodded Old Father Christmas.

"My father says you're eighteen hundred and thirty years old," I whispered.

"Aye, aye, to be sure," said Old Father Christmas. "I'm a long age."

"A very long age!" I said to myself. And then I said to him, "You're the oldest man in the world, you know," in case he hadn't thought of that.

"Aye, aye," said Father Christmas, and nodded a lot, but he didn't really seem to think anything of it. After a bit he held up the tree and said, "D'you know what this is, little Miss?"

"A Christmas tree," said Patty.

And the old man smiled and nodded.

I leaned over the wall and shouted, "But there aren't any candles!"

"By-and-by," said Father Christmas, nodding away again. "When it's dark they'll all be lit up. That'll be a fine sight!"

"There'll be toys too, won't there?" screamed Patty.

Father Christmas nodded his head. "And sweeties!" He licked his lips.

I could feel Patty trembling beside me, and my own

heart was beating fast. What we were so eager to know was this – was Father Christmas bringing the tree to us? But that was what we daren't ask him. What if he wasn't!

At last he put the tree over his shoulders again and started to move away, and I shouted out in despair, "Oh, you're not going, are you?"

"I'm coming back soon," he said.

"How soon?" Patty shouted.

"About four o'clock," said the old man, smiling. "I'm only going up yonder."

And off he went, nodding and chuckling, down the snowy lane, and behind him there crept a little brown and white spaniel, looking very dirty in the snow.

Up yonder!

What was that supposed to mean? Father Christmas had pointed vaguely upwards, but it could have meant anywhere, up in the field, or in the squire's woods, or up in the sky even. It could have been anywhere.

"Where's up yonder?" asked Patty.

I was as puzzled as she was. "I think it must be in Squire's woods," I told her. "Maybe Old Father Christmas has got a cave up there, like Aladdin's cave probably, and that's where he gets the candles and all the pretty things for the tree."

"I wonder if he's got something for us!" said Patty.

So we started to walk back home, full of thoughts of the wonderful cave where Father Christmas decorated his Christmas trees.

"Patty," I said. "I wonder why there's no picture of Father Christmas's dog in the book?"

"Perhaps it's a new dog that he's got to guard his cave," said Patty.

When we went indoors we opened the picture book again and looked at it in the dim light from the passage window, but there was no dog there.

At that moment my father passed me and patted my head.

"I'm not sure," I said to him, "but I think Father Christmas might be going to bring us a Christmas tree tonight."

"Who's been telling you that?" he said, but he had gone before I had the chance to explain that we had seen Father Christmas himself, and had had his word for it that he would come back at four o'clock, and that the candles on the tree would be lit as soon as it was dark.

We hung about outside the rooms till four o'clock came. We sat on the stairs and watched the big clock. I had just learnt to tell the time, but Patty made herself dizzy by looking up every other second to watch the big hand on its slow way towards the figure four. We put our noses into the kitchen now and then to smell the cakes baking and to get warm. Sometimes we hung around the parlour door.

"Stop peeping!" our mother called to us.

But what did we care what she was doing in the parlour? Hadn't we seen Old Father Christmas himself, and weren't we expecting him back again at any minute!

At last the church clock struck. The sounds boomed heavily through the frost, and Patty thought there were four of them. Then our own clock started choking and

whirring and at last it struck, and we counted the notes quite clearly – one! two! three! four! We ran to get Kitty's cloak again and stole out into the backyard. We ran up to our old place, and peeped, but couldn't see anything.

"We'd better get up on to the wall," I said. Patty struggled up, rubbing her bare knees on the cold stones and getting snow up her sleeves. I was just beginning to scramble after her when something cold and something warm came suddenly against the bare calves of my legs and I yelled with fright. I tumbled down and bruised my knees, my elbows and my chin, and the snow that hadn't gone up Patty's sleeves went down my neck. Then I found that the cold thing was a dog's nose, and the warm thing was his tongue.

"It's Father Christmas's dog, and he's licking your legs," said Patty.

It really was that dirty little brown and white spaniel, and he kept on and on licking me and jumping on me, and making funny little noises as if he was trying to say something to me if only I could speak his language. I didn't know what to do, I can tell you. My legs were hurting, and I was a bit frightened of the dog, and Patty was very frightened of sitting on the wall without me.

"You won't fall. Hold on," I said to her.

And, "Go away!" I said to the jumping dog.

"Humpty Dumpty fell off a wall," said Patty.

"Bow! Wow!" said the dog.

I pulled Patty down, and the dog tried to pull me down; but when my little sister was on her feet I was quite glad to see that he was more interested in her than he was in me. He jumped up and licked her a few times, and then he turned round and ran away.

"He's gone!" I said. "Thank goodness for that."

But there he was, back again, crouching at Patty's

feet and glaring at her with eyes that were the same muddy colour as his ears.

Now Patty was very fond of animals, and when the dog looked at her she looked at the dog, and then she said to me, "He wants us to go with him."

He understood that all right. He sprang up and away from us and ran off as fast as he could, and Patty and I ran after him. I had a faint hope at the back of my mind,

"Perhaps Father Christmas has sent him to fetch us," I thought.

And sure enough, the dog led us up the lane. But only a little way. He stopped by something that was lying in the ditch, and once more we said in the same breath,

"It's Old Father Christmas."

· CHAPTER FOUR ·

THE CHRISTMAS TREE

Patty began to cry.

"I think he's dead," she sobbed.

"He is very old," I whispered. "Eighteen hundred and thirty. It wouldn't surprise me, Patty. But I'll go and fetch help."

My father and Kitty came out straight away. They thought that the old man had slipped on the ice on his way down from the Hall, and had knocked himself out for a bit. Kitty was as strong as any man; they carried him between them into the kitchen. He soon came round. Kitty was marvellous. She didn't complain once that her work had been interrupted. She pulled the old man's chair close to the fire, and she even let his little dog go right up to the hearth. As soon as Puss saw this she lay down with her back snuggled up so close to the spaniel's that Kitty would have had to kick them both out if she wanted to get rid of her.

If Patty and I hadn't been so worried about the tree we would have thought it was a wonderful treat to sit in the kitchen having tea with Old Father Christmas. And what a tea it was! Usually we had bread and treacle, but tonight we had all the bits and pieces of cakes and biscuits that had gone wrong in the oven, and the leftover bits of pastry and the 'tasters and wasters', as Kitty called them, that had only been put into the oven to test that it was hot enough for the real thing.

And there we sat, helping Old Father Christmas to tea and cake and wondering in our hearts what could have happened to the tree. We just didn't dare to ask him about it. It wasn't until we'd had three cups of tea each, with tasters and wasters every time, that Patty said very gently,

"It's quite dark now." And then she heaved a deep sigh.

I couldn't stop myself. I leaned towards Father Christmas and shouted, "I suppose the candles are all on the tree now?"

"Just about," said Father Christmas.

"And the presents too?" said Patty.

"Aye, aye, to be sure," said Father Christmas, with his wonderful smile.

I was trying to think what else I dared ask him when he pushed his cup towards Patty, saying, "Since you insist, Miss, I'll have another cup."

And Kitty, swooping on us from the oven, cried,

"Make yourself at home, Sir! There's more where these came from. Stretch your arm out, Miss Patty, and hand them cakes round."

So Patty did as she was told and handed Old Father Christmas the plate of cakes, and then she picked up the teapot and, holding the lid with one hand and pouring with the other, filled up his cup. Our hearts were heavy, I can tell you.

But at last he was finished. We all stood up to say grace after meals, but he stayed with his eyes tight shut long after I'd said Amen, – I think he was so deaf that he hadn't heard a word of it. And just as he was sitting down again my father put his head round the kitchen door. This is what he said:

"Old Father Christmas has sent a tree to the children."

Patty and I shouted with joy and danced round the old man saying, "Oh, how lovely! Oh, how kind of you!" which I think must have puzzled him, but he only smiled and nodded.

"Come along," my father said. "Come on, children. Come on Kitty. And Reuben."

And he went into the parlour, and we all followed him.

And there was the tree.

My godmother's picture of a Christmas tree was very pretty; and the flames of the candles looked so real painted in red and yellow that I always wondered why

they didn't shine in the dark. But the picture was nowhere near as wonderful as the real thing.

We had been sitting almost in the dark in the kitchen, because Kitty always said that firelight was good enough to burn at mealtimes. And then the parlour door was thrown open, and the tree with all its flickering candles burst into view. The blaze was dazzling. It threw such a glory of light round the little gifts, and round the coloured hanging bags of acid drops and pink rose drops, and liquorice comfits, that I shall never forget the sight of it.

We all got something, and Patty and I were quite sure that everything had come from Old Father Christmas's hidden cave. My father came in with a bundle of old clothes and handed them to him.

"Here you are, Reuben. We can't forget you, can we?"

And even when the old man smiled and nodded and shuffled out into the snow with his present under his arm, we still believed he had given us the tree.

We were all very happy, even Kitty, though she kept her sleeves rolled up and didn't quite like to be seen enjoying herself. Busy people are often like that. She went back to her oven before the Christmas tree lights were put out; even before the angel on the top had been taken down and given to Patty. She locked away her present at once. It was a little wooden work-box. She often showed it off afterwards, but she kept it wrapped in the same bit of tissue paper till the day she died. Our presents didn't last so long, you can be sure of that!

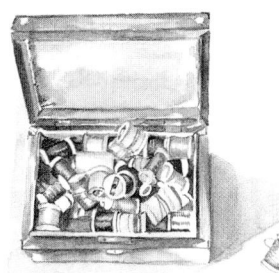

The old man died about a week later. His little dog came to live with us. I suppose he remembered how warm our kitchen was. Patty was his special friend, but he seemed very fond of all of us. Puss seemed to like him too.

And when we took him for walks, rambling round the fields in summer time, I always hoped that he would lead us to the cave where Christmas tree candles and presents are hidden. But he never did.

Our mother and father often talked about the old man. They called him 'Old Reuben'.

But to Patty and me he was Old Father Christmas, and he always will be.

For Liz Cashdan
With thanks to Gina Pollinger
BD

In Memory of John Brain
For the families
Fattorini and Zeeman
And for my own family
MTM

JULIANA HORATIA EWING

Juliana Horatia Ewing was born in 1841 in Eccles-field, Yorkshire, the second of nine children. Her mother, Margaret Gatty, was a successful children's writer and had a great influence on her daughter's life. From a very early age, Juliana Ewing displayed a vivid imagination and an aptitude for storytelling, which her mother actively encouraged.

She began her writing career well before her marriage to Alexander Ewing in 1867 when she was 26. Her numerous children's stories appeared in periodicals before being published in book form. She continued to write throughout her adult life until her death in 1885 at the age of 44.

Like many of her contemporaries, she chose to write about large, happy families. But Mrs Ewing went beyond the conventions of the day by conveying family affection and happy moments of childhood, without moralizing. *Old Father Christmas* is an ideal example of her unique ability to reveal the intense, yet simple joy that Christmas brings for children.